John Davidson

New Ballads

Second Edition

John Davidson

New Ballads
Second Edition

ISBN/EAN: 9783744766364

Printed in Europe, USA, Canada, Australia, Japan

Cover: Foto ©Andreas Hilbeck / pixelio.de

More available books at **www.hansebooks.com**

NEW BALLADS

BY
JOHN DAVIDSON

JOHN LANE
THE BODLEY HEAD
LONDON & NEW YORK
1897

Second Edition

CONTENTS

Some said, 'He was strong.'   He was weak ;
For he never could sing or speak
Of the things beneath or the things above,
Till his soul was touched by death or love.

Some said, 'He was weak.'   They were wrong;
For the soul must be strong
That can break into song
Of the things beneath and the things above,
At the stroke of death, at the touch of love.

A BALLAD OF AN ARTIST'S WIFE

'Sweet wife, this heavy-hearted age
  Is nought to us ; we two shall look
To Art, and fill a perfect page
  In Life's ill-written doomsday book.'

He wrought in colour ; blood and brain
  Gave fire and might ; and beauty grew
And flowered with every magic stain
  His passion on the canvas threw.

They shunned the world and worldly ways :
  He laboured with a constant will ;
But few would look, and none would praise,
  Because of something lacking still.

After a time her days with sighs
  And tears o'erflowed ; for blighting need
Bedimmed the lustre of her eyes,
  And there were little mouths to feed.

' My bride shall ne'er be common-place,
  He thought, and glanced; and glanced again :
At length he looked her in the face ;
  And lo, a woman old and plain !

About this time the world's heart failed—
  The lusty heart no fear could rend ;
In every land wild voices wailed,
  And prophets prophesied the end.

' To-morrow or to-day,' he thought,
  ' May be Eternity ; and I
Have neither felt nor fashioned aught
  That makes me unconcerned to die.

' With care and counting of the cost

My life a sterile waste has grown,

Wherein my better dreams are lost

Like chaff in the Sahara sown.

' I must escape this living tomb !

My life shall yet be rich and free,

And on the very stroke of Doom

My soul at last begin to be.

' Wife, children, duty, household fires

For victims of the good and true !

For me my infinite desires,

Freedom and things untried and new !

' I would encounter all the press

Of thought and feeling life can show,

The sweet embrace, the aching stress

Of every earthly joy and woe ;

' And from the world's impending wreck
  And out of pain and pleasure weave
Beauty undreamt of, to bedeck
  The Festival of Doomsday Eve.'

He fled, and joined a motley throng
  That held carousal day and night;
With love and wit, with dance and song,
  They snatched a last intense delight.

Passion to mould an age's art,
  Enough to keep a century sweet,
Was in an hour consumed ; each heart
  Lavished a life in every beat.

Amazing beauty filled the looks
  Of sleepless women ; music bore
New wonder on its wings ; and books
  Throbbed with a thought unknown before.

The sun began to smoke and flare
    Like a spent lamp about to die ;
The dusky moon tarnished the air ;
    The planets withered in the sky.

Earth reeled and lurched upon her road ;
    Tigers were cowed, and wolves grew tame ;
Seas shrank, and rivers backward flowed,
    And mountain-ranges burst in flame.

The artist's wife, a soul devout,
    To all these things gave little heed ;
For though the sun was going out,
    There still were little mouths to feed.

And there were also shrouds to stitch,
    And chares to do ; with all her might,
To feed her babes, she served the rich
    And kept her useless tears till night.

But by-and-by her sight grew dim ;

   Her strength gave way ; in desperate mood

She laid her down to die. ' Tell him,'

   She sighed, ' I fed them while I could.'

The children met a wretched fate ;

   Self-love was all the vogue and vaunt,

And charity gone out of date ;

   Wherefore they pined and died of want.

Aghast he heard the story : ' Dead !

   All dead in hunger and despair !

I courted misery,' he said ;

   ' But here is more than I can bear.'

Then, as he wrought, the stress of woe

   Appeared in many a magic stain ;

And all adored his work, for lo,

   Tears mingled now with blood and brain !

' Look, look ! ' they cried ; ' this man can weave

    Beauty from anguish that appals ; '

And at the feast of Doomsday Eve

    They hung his pictures in their halls,

And gazed ; and came again between

    The faltering dances eagerly ;

They said, ' The loveliest we have seen,

    The last, of man's work, we shall see ! '

Then was there neither death nor birth ;

    Time ceased ; and through the ether fell

The smoky sun, the leprous earth—

    A cinder and an icicle.

No wrathful vials were unsealed ;

    Silent, the first things passed away :

No terror reigned ; no trumpet pealed

    The dawn of Everlasting Day.

The bitter draught of sorrow's cup
    Passed with the seasons and the years ;
And Wisdom dried for ever up
    The deep, old fountainhead of tears.

Out of the grave and ocean's bed
    The artist saw the people rise ;
And all the living and the dead
    Were borne aloft to Paradise.

He came where on a silver throne
    A spirit sat for ever young ;
Before her Seraphs worshipped prone,
    And Cherubs silver censers swung.

He asked, ' Who may this martyr be ?
    What votaress of saintly rule ? '
A Cherub said, ' No martyr ; she
    Had one gift ; she was beautiful.'

Then came he to another bower

Where one sat on a golden seat,

Adored by many a heavenly Power

With golden censers smoking sweet.

' This was some gallant wench who led

Faint-hearted folk and set them free ? '

' Oh no ! a simple maid,' they said,

' Who spent her life in charity.'

At last he reached a mansion blest

Where on a diamond throne, endued

With nameless beauty, one possessed

Ineffable beatitude.

The praises of this matchless soul

The sons of God proclaimed aloud ;

From diamond censers odours stole ;

And Hierarchs before her bowed.

'Who was she?' God Himself replied :

'In misery her lot was cast ;

She lived a woman's life, and died

Working My work until the last.'

It was his wife. He said, 'I pray

Thee, Lord, despatch me now to Hell.'

But God said, 'No; here shall you stay,

And in her peace for ever dwell.'

SPRING SONG

About the flowerless land adventurous bees
    Pickeering hum ; the rooks debate, divide,
    With many a hoarse aside,
In solemn conclave on the budding trees;
Larks in the skies and ploughboys o'er the leas
Carol as if the winter ne'er had been ;
    The very owl comes out to greet the sun ;
    Rivers high-hearted run ;
And hedges mantle with a flush of green.

The curlew calls me where the salt winds blow;
    His troubled note dwells mournfully and dies;
    Then the long echo cries

Deep in my heart.   Ah, surely I must go !

For there the tides, moon-haunted, ebb and

    flow ;

And there the seaboard murmurs resonant ;

  The waves their interwoven fugue repeat

  And brooding surges beat

A slow, melodious, continual chant.

A NORTHERN SUBURB

NATURE selects the longest way,
    And winds about in tortuous grooves ;
A thousand years the oaks decay ;
    The wrinkled glacier hardly moves.

But here the whetted fangs of change
    Daily devour the old demesne—
The busy farm, the quiet grange,
    The wayside inn, the village green.

In gaudy yellow brick and red,
    With rooting pipes, like creepers rank,
The shoddy terraces o'erspread
    Meadow, and garth, and daisied bank.

With shelves for rooms the houses crowd,

    Like draughty cupboards in a row—

Ice-chests when wintry winds are loud,

    Ovens when summer breezes blow.

Roused by the fee'd policeman's knock,

    And sad that day should come again,

Under the stars the workmen flock

    In haste to reach the workmen's train.

For here dwell those who must fulfil

    Dull tasks in uncongenial spheres,

Who toil through dread of coming ill,

    And not with hope of happier years—

The lowly folk who scarcely dare

    Conceive themselves perhaps misplaced,

Whose prize for unremitting care

    Is only not to be disgraced.

A WOMAN AND HER SON

'HAS he come yet?' the dying woman asked.

'No,' said the nurse.   'Be quiet.'

                              'When he comes
Bring him to me: I may not live an hour.'

'Not if you talk.   Be quiet.'

                              'When he comes
Bring him to me.'

                         'Hush, will you!'

                         Night came down.
The cries of children playing in the street

Suddenly rose more voluble and shrill;

Ceased, and broke out again; and ceased and broke

In eager prate; then dwindled and expired.

' Across the dreary common once I saw

The moon rise out of London like a ghost.

Has the moon risen ?   Is he come ? '

                         ' Not yet.

Be still, or you will die before he comes.'

The working-men with heavy iron tread,

The thin-shod clerks, the shopmen neat and plump

Home from the city came.   On muddy beer

The melancholy mean suburban street

Grew maudlin for an hour; pianos waked

In dissonance from dreams of rusty peace,

And unpitched voices quavered tedious songs
Of sentiment infirm or nerveless mirth.

'Has he come yet?'

        'Be still or you will die!'

And when the hour of gaiety had passed,
And the poor revellers were gone to bed,
The moon among the chimneys wandering long
Escaped at last, and sadly overlooked
The waste raw land where doleful suburbs thrive.

Then came a firm quick step—measured but
      quick;
And then a triple knock that shook the house
And brought the plaster down.

        'My son!' she cried.
'Bring him to me!'

He came ; the nurse went out.

' Mother, I thought to spare myself this pain,'
He said at once, ' but that was cowardly.
And so I come to bid you try to think,
To understand at last.'

' Still hard, my son ? '

' Hard as the nether millstone.'

' But I hope
To soften you,' she said, ' before I die.'

' And I to see you harden with a hiss
As life goes out in the cold bath of death.
Oh, surely now your creed will set you free
For one great moment, and the universe
Flash on your intellect as power, power, power,
Knowing not good or evil, God or sin,

But only everlasting yea and nay.

Is weakness greatness ?   No, a thousand times !

Is force the greatest ?   Yes, for ever yes !

Be strong, be great, now you have come to die.'

' My son, you seem to me a kind of prig.'

' How can I get it said ?   Think, mother, think !

Look back upon your fifty wretched years

And show me anywhere the hand of God.

Your husband saving souls—O, paltry souls

That need salvation !—lost the grip of things,

And left you penniless with none to aid

But me the prodigal.   Back to the start !

An orphan girl, hurt, melancholy, frail,

Before you learned to play, your toil began:

That might have been your making, had the
        weight

Of drudgery, the unsheathed fire of woe

Borne down and beat on your defenceless life :

Souls shrivel up in these extremes of pain,

Or issue diamonds to engrave the world ;

But yours before it could be made or marred,

Plucked from the burning, saved by faith,

    became

Inferior as a thing of paste that hopes

To pass for real in heaven's enduing light.

You married then a crude evangelist,

Whose soul was like a wafer that can take

One single impress only.'

                ' Oh, my son !

Your father ! '

              ' He, my father ! These are times

When all must to the crucible—no thought,

Practice, or use, or custom sacro-sanct

But shall be violable now.   And first

If ever we evade the wonted round,

The stagnant vortex of the eddying years,

The child must take the father by the beard,

And say, " What did you in begetting me ? " '

' I will not listen ! '

     ' But you shall, you must—

You cannot help yourself.   Death in your eyes

And voice, and I to torture you with truth,

Even as your preachers for a thousand years

Pestered with falsehood souls of dying folk.

Look at the man, your husband.   Of the soil;

Broad, strong, adust; head, massive; eyes of steel;

Yet some way ailing, for he understood

But one idea, and he married you.'

The dying woman sat up straight in bed;

A ghastly blush glowed on her yellow cheek,

And flame broke from her eyes, but words came

> not.

The son's pent wrath burnt on. 'He married

> you;

You were his wife, his servant; cheerfully

You bore him children; and your house was hell.

Unwell, half-starved, and clad in cast-off clothes,

We had no room, no sport; nothing but fear

Of our evangelist, whose little purse

Opened to all save us; who squandered smiles

On wily proselytes, and gloomed at home.

You had eight children; only three grew up :

Of these, one died bedrid, and one insane,

And I alone am left you.   Think of it !

It matters nothing if a fish, a plant

Teem with waste offspring, but a conscious womb !

Eight times you bore a child, and in fierce throes,

For you were frail and small: of all your love,

Your hopes, your passion, not a memory steals

To smooth your dying pillow, only I

Am here to rack you.   Where does God appear?'

'God shall appear,' the dying woman said.

'God has appeared ; my heart is in his hand.

Were there no God, no Heaven!—Oh, foolish
    boy!

You foolish fellow!   Pain and trouble here

Are God's benignest providence—the whip

And spur to Heaven.   But joy was mine below—

I am unjust to God—great joy was mine :

Which makes Heaven sweeter too ; because if
    earth

Afford such pleasure in mortality

What must immortal happiness be like!

Eight times I was a mother. Frail and small ?

Yes ; but the passionate, courageous mate

Of a strong man. Oh, boy ! You paltry boy !

Hush ! Think ! Think—you ! Eight times I

    bore a child,

Eight souls for God ! In Heaven they wait for me—

My husband and the seven. I see them all !

And two are children still—my little ones !

While I have sorrowed here, shrinking sometimes

From that which was decreed, my Father, God,

Was storing Heaven with treasure for me. Hush!

My dowry in the skies ! God's thoughtfulness !

I see it all ! Lest Heaven might, unalloyed,

Distress my shy soul, I leave earth in doubt

Of your salvation : something to hope and fear

Until I get accustomed to the peace

That passeth understanding. When you come—

For you will come, my son. . . .'

Her strength gave out ;
She sank down panting, bathed in tears and
sweat.

' Could I but touch your intellect,' he cried,
' Before you die ! Mother, the world is mad :
This castle in the air, this Heaven of yours,
Is the lewd dream of morbid vanity.
For each of us death is the end of all ;
And when the sun goes out the race of men
Shall cease for ever. It is ours to make
This farce of fate a splendid tragedy :
Since we must be the sport of circumstance,
We should be sportsmen, and produce a breed
Of gallant creatures, conscious of their doom,
Marching with lofty brows, game to the last.
Oh good and evil, heaven and hell are lies !
But strength is great : there is no other truth :

This is the yea-and-nay that makes men hard.

Mother, be hard and happy in your death.'

' What do you say ?   I hear the waters roll. . .'

Then, with a faint cry, striving to arise—

' After I die I shall come back to you,

And then you must believe ; you must believe,

For I shall bring you news of God and Heaven ! '

He set his teeth, and saw his mother die.

Outside a city-reveller's tipsy tread

Severed the silence with a jagged rent ;

The tall lamps flickered through the sombre
        street,

With yellow light hiding the stainless stars :

In the next house a child awoke and cried ;

Far off a clank and clash of shunting trains

Broke out and ceased, as if the fettered world

C

Started and shook its irons in the night ;

Across the dreary common citywards,

The moon, among the chimneys sunk again,

Cast on the clouds a shade of smoky pearl.

And when her funeral day had come, her son,

Before they fastened down the coffin lid,

Shut himself in the chamber, there to gaze

Upon her dead face, hardening his heart.

But as he gazed, into the smooth wan cheek

Life with its wrinkles shot again ; the eyes

Burst open, and the bony fingers clutched

The coffin sides ; the woman raised herself,

And owl-like in her shroud blinked on the light.

'Mother, what news of God and Heaven ?' he
     asked.

Feeble and strange, her voice came from afar :

' I am not dead : I must have been asleep.'

' Do not imagine that.   You lay here dead—

Three days and nights, a corpse.   Life has come

    back :

Often it does, although faint-hearted folk

Fear to admit it : none of those who die,

And come to life again, can ever tell

Of any bourne from which they have returned :

Therefore they were not dead, your casuists say.

The ancient jugglery that tricks the world !

You lay here dead, three days and nights.   What

    news ?

" After I die I shall come back to you,

And then you must believe "—these were your

    words—

" For I shall bring you news of God and Heaven." '

She cast a look forlorn about the room :

The door was shut ; the worn venetian, down ;

And stuffy sunlight through the dusty slats

Spotted the floor, and smeared the faded walls.

He with his strident voice and eyes of steel

Stood by relentless.

                              ' I remember, dear,'

She whispered, ' very little.   When I died

I saw my children dimly bending down,

The little ones in front, to beckon me,

A moment in the dark ; and that is all.'

' That was before you died—the last attempt

Of fancy to create the heart's desire.

Now mother, be courageous ; now, be hard.'

' What must I say or do, my dearest son ?

Oh me, the deep discomfort of my mind !

Come to me, hold me, help me to be brave,

And I shall make you happy if I can,

For I have none but you—none anywhere . . .

Mary, the youngest, whom you never saw

Looked out of Heaven first: her little hands. . . .

Three days and nights, dead, and no memory ! . . .

A poor old creature dying a second death,

I understand the settled treachery,

The plot of love and hope against the world.

Fearless, I gave myself at nature's call ;

And when they died, my children, one by one,

All sweetly in my heart I buried them.

Who stole them while I slept ?   Where are
     they all ?

My heart is eerie, like a rifled grave

Where silent spiders spin among the dust,

And the wind moans and laughs under its
     breath.

But in a drawer. . . . What is there in the
    drawer?

No pressure of a little rosy hand

Upon a faded cheek—nor anywhere

The seven fair stars I made. Oh love the cheat !

And hope, the radiant devil pointing up,

Lest men should cease to give the couple sport

And end the world at once ! For three days
    dead—

Here in my coffin ; and no memory !

Oh, it is hard ! But I—I, too, am hard . . .

Be hard, my son, and steep your heart of flesh

In stony waters till it grows a stone,

Or love and hope will hack it with blunt knives

As long as it can feel.'

                        He, holding her,

With sobs and laughter spoke : his mind had
    snapped

Like a frayed string o'erstretched : 'Mother,
    rejoice ;

For I shall make you glad.   There is no
    heaven

Your children are resolved to dust and dew :

But, mother, I am God.   I shall create

The heaven of your desires.   There must be
    heaven

For mothers and their babes.   Let heaven be
    now !'

They found him conjuring chaos with mad
    words

And brandished hands across his mother's
    corpse.

Thus did he see her harden with a hiss

As life went out in the cold bath of death ;

Thus did she soften him before she died :

For both were bigots—fateful souls that plague

The gentle world.

A SONG OF THE ROAD

AMONG the hills he woke ;
 A star, low-hung and late,
Dwindled as the morning broke
 The sable-silvered state
Wherein night braves the ruddy stroke
 That daily seals her fate.

He went by bank and brae
 Where fern and heather spread ;
Azure bells beset the way,
 And blossoms gold and red ;
Below, the burn sang all the day ;
 The larks sang overhead.

He left the hills and came
    Among the woods and dells ;
Golden helmets flashed like flame ;
    The witches wove their spells ;
In moss-green silk the elfin dame
    Rode by with silver bells.

He came where four roads met ;
    He chose a narrow one ;
Spiny thorns the way beset ;
    But at the end there shone
The bright reward that pilgrims get,
    And Heaven's unsetting sun.

He went with heavy mind,
    For sharp the thorns did sting.
Far and fitfully behind
    He heard sweet laughter ring—

Delighted voices on the wind,

   And freshness of the spring.

He paused in sore dismay,

   And, pondering right and wrong,

Turned and left the narrow way

   To join the pleasant throng,

That wandered happily astray

   The primrose path along.

Alas! he fled once more;

   For at the end a cloud,

Streaked with flame, and stained with gore,

   And torn with curses loud,

O'erhung a melancholy shore

   And veiled a hopeless crowd.

He followed then the road

   Wherein at first he hied;

Soon he came where men abode

And loved, and wrought, and died ;

And straight the Broad and Narrow ways,

Heaven fair and Hell obscene,

For ever vanished out of space,

Spectres that ne'er had been.

A HIGHWAY PIMPERNEL

Blossoms and buds, purple or pale,
  In saffron kerchiefs or watchet snoods,
Linger in ditches, crowd in the dale,
  In passionate tempers, or languorous moods,
High on the hill, deep in the vale,
  Over the fences and into the woods !

Richer and sweeter far than the rest,
  On the edge of the rut the cart-wheels chafe,
Like a fairy-buoy on a billow's crest,
  Hangs a wonderful little waif :
A pimpernel, clutching the earth's warm breast,
  Rocked by the traffic and sleeping safe.

All the morning in crimson state

   It flashed and glowed with zeal entire.

All the morning, steady as fate,

   Aflame with courage and high desire,

It watched the sun, its skyey mate,

   Lighting the world with golden fire.

But not a petal now will budge—

   Fast asleep since the stroke of noon !

And weary beggar and hawker trudge

   Grazing its leaves with their mouldy shoon,

And wheels and hoofs go by with a grudge

   To think that a flower should rest so soon !

A BALLAD OF EUTHANASIA

In magic books she read at night,
    And found all things to be
A spectral pageant brought to light
    By nameless sorcery.

' Bethink you, now, my daughter dear,'
    The King of Norway cried,
' 'Tis summer, and your twentieth year—
    High time you were a bride !

' The sunlight lingers o'er the wold
    By night ; the stars above
With passion throb like hearts of gold ;
    The whole world is in love.'

The scornful princess laughed and said,

' This love you praise, I hate.

Oh, I shall never, never wed;

For men degenerate.

' The sun grows dim on heaven's brow;

The world's worn blood runs cold;

Time staggers in his dotage now;

Nature is growing old.

' Deluded by the summertime,

Must I with wanton breath

Whisper and sigh ?   I trow not !—I

Shall be the bride of Death.'

Fair princes came with gems of price,

And kings from lands afar.

' Jewels !' she said.   ' I may not wed

Till Death comes with a star.'

A BALLAD OF EUTHANASIA

At midnight when she ceased to read,
  She pushed her lattice wide,
And saw the crested rollers lead
  The vanguard of the tide.

The mighty host of waters swayed,
  Commanded by the moon;
The wind a marching music made;
  The surges chimed in tune.

But she with sudden-startled ears
  O'erheard a ghostly sound—
Or drums that beat, or trampling feet,
  Above or underground.

The mountain-side was girt about
  With forests dark and deep.
' What meteor flashes in and out
  Thridding the darksome steep ? '

D

Soon light and sound reached level ground,
    And lo, in blackest mail,
Along the shore a warrior
    Rode on a war-horse pale !

And from his helm as on he came
    A crescent lustre gleamed;
The charger's hoofs were shod with flame :
    The wet sand hissed and steamed.

' He leaves me ! Nay ; he turns this way
    From elfin lands afar.
' 'Tis Death ! ' she said. ' He comes to wed
    His true love with a star !

' No ring for me, no blushing groom,
    No love with all its ills,
No long-drawn life ! I am the wife
    Of Death, whose first kiss kills.'

The rider reached the city wall ;

  Over the gate he dashed ;

Across the roofs the fire-shod hoofs

  Like summer-lightning flashed.

Before her bower the pale horse pawed

  The air, unused to rest ;

The sable groom, he whispered 'Come ! '

  And stooped his shining crest.

She sprang behind him ; on her brow

  He placed his glowing star.

Back o'er the roofs the fire-shod hoofs

  Like lightning flashed afar.

Through hissing sand and shrivelled grass

  And flowers singed and dead,

By wood and lea, by stream and sea,

  The pale horse panting sped.

At last as they beheld the morn
　　His sovereignty resume,
Deep in an ancient land forlorn
　　They reached a marble tomb.

They lighted down and entered in :
　　The tears, they brimmed her eyes ;
She turned and took a lingering look,
　　A last look at the skies ;

Then went with Death.　Her lambent star
　　The sullen darkness lit
In avenues of sombre yews,
　　Where ghosts did peer and flit.

But soon the way grew light as day;
　　With wonderment and awe,
A golden land, a silver strand,
　　And grass-green hills she saw.

In gown and smock good country folk
　In fields and meadows worked;
The salt seas wet the ruddy net
　Where glistering fishes lurked.

The meads were strewn with purple flowers,
　With every flower that blows;
And singing loud o'er cliff and cloud
　The larks, the larks arose!

'The sun is bright on heaven's brow,
　The world's fresh blood runs fleet;
Time is as young as ever now,
　Nature as fresh and sweet,'

Her champion said; then through the wood
　He led her to a bower;
He doffed his sable casque and stood
　A young man in his flower!

'Lo! I am Life, your lover true!'
    He kissed her o'er and o'er.
And still she wist not what to do,
    And still she wondered more.

And they were wed.   The swift years sped
    Till children's children laughed ;
And joy and pain and joy again
    Mixed in the cup they quaffed.

Upon their golden wedding day,
    He said, ' How now, dear wife ? '
Then she : ' I find the sweetest kind
    Of Death is Love and Life,'

SUNSET

By down and shore the South-west bore
 The scent of hay, an airy load :
As if at fault it seemed to halt,
 Then, softly whispering, took the road,
To haunt the evening like a ghost,
Or some belated pilgrim lost.

High overhead the slow clouds sped ;
 Beside the moon they furled their sails;
Soon in the skies their merchandise
 Of vapour, built in toppling bales,
Fulfilled a visionary pier
That spanned the eastern atmosphere.

Low in the west the sun addressed

　　His courtship to the dark-browed night;

While images of molten seas,

　　Of snowy slope and crimson height,

Of valleys dim and gulfs profound

Aloft a dazzling pageant wound.

Where shadows fell in glade and dell

　　Uncovered shoulders nestled deep,

And here and there the braided hair

　　Of rosy goddesses asleep ;

For in a moment clouds may be

Dead, and instinct with deity.

WINTER RAIN

MOTIONLESS, leaden cloud
  The region roofed and walled ;
Beneath, a tempest shrieked aloud,
  And the forest beckoned and called.

The blackthorn coppice was all ablaze,
  And shot and garlanded,
With bronzed and wreathing bramble sprays,
  And bright leaves green and red.

The dripping pollards their shock-heads hung,
  And in the glistening shaws,
Lustres and glories of rubies, swung
  The dark wet crimson haws.

The dead leaves pattered and stole about
    Like elves in the sheltered glades,
And rushed down the broad green rides and out
    O'er the fields in windy raids.

The motionless, leaden sky,
    Emptied itself amain,
And the angry east with hue and cry
    Dashed at the pouring rain.

The forest rocked and sang :
    Behind the passing blast
Far off the new blast faintly rang
    Arrived and roared, and passed,
In the liberty of the open sea
    To find a home at last.

A BALLAD OF A POET BORN

Upon a ruddy ember eve
  They feasted in the hall;
By custom bound they handed round
  The harp to each and all.

While still the smoky rafters rang
  With burdens loud and long,
There rose a blushing youth and sang
  A wonderful new song.

For he had lounged among the flowers,
  Beside the mountain streams,
Deep-dyeing all the rosy hours
  With rosier waking dreams.

And lurked at night in seaside caves,

Or rowed o'er harbour-bars,

Companion of the winds and waves

Companion of the stars.

Therefore as searching-sweet as musk

The words were and the tune,

The while he sang of dawn and dusk,

Of midnight and of noon.

' No longer shall more gifted lands

Cast hither words of scorn.

Behold!' they said, and clapped their hands,

' We have a poet⸗born !

' Go forth with harp and scrip,' they cried,

' And sing by land and sea,

In lanes and streets; the world is wide

For errant minstrelsy.

' Accept their lot in every clime
    Who win the poet's name,
  Homeless and poor, but rich in rhyme,
    And glittering with fame.'

' Forth would I go without all fear,
    Gladly to meet my fate;
  But in the house my mother dear
    And my three sisters wait.

' My father's dead; my mother's eyes
    Are overcast with woe;
  I hear my sisters' hungry cries;
    I dare not rise and go.'

  They jeered him for a craven lout :
    ' What care is this of thine ?
  Thou speakest now, without a doubt,
    Like some false Philistine !

'No poet can to others give :
  Leave folk to starve alone.'
He said, 'I dare not while I live
  She has no other son.'

His sweetheart whispered in his ear
  'And me, love ! what of me ?'
He shook her off. 'Of you, enough,'
  He sighed; 'I set you free.'

He herded sheep, he herded kine;
  He rose before the day;
He ploughed and sowed and reaped and mowed,
  To keep the wolf at bay.

His harp, it rusted on the wall;
  His hands, his heart, grew hard;
The wine of life was turned to gall
  Because the song was marred.

So stubborn the accursed soil,

   So poor his pastoral lore,

With all his weary task and toil

   The wolf still pawed the door.

His mother died uncomforted;

   His sisters, one by one,

By beggars born were wooed and wed,

   And all his hopes undone.

Haggard and worn he took his harp;

   The sun shone broad and low :

' At dawn of night there shall be light;

   I now may rise and go.'

As he went o'er the plain he met

   The sweetheart of his youth :

' Whither away at close of day ?

   Now answer me in sooth.'

' My kin have left me; it is time
　　To win the poet's name;
　Homeless and poor, but rich in rhyme,
　　I go to conquer fame.'

' Oh, once you throned me in your heart
　　All other maids above;
　Sing to me here, before we part,
　　Your sweetest song of love.'

He said, ' I'll play and sing a lay
　　The sweetest ever sung.'
Then fumbled with his knotted hands
　　The rusty strings among.

His quivering lips gave forth no song,
　　His harp no silver sound ;
Deep like a boy he blushed, and long
　　He looked upon the ground.

He gnashed his teeth : 'Hell has begun,'
　He thought; 'I feel its blaze.'
With that he faced the setting sun,
　And then the woman's gaze.

' We two,' she said, ' must never part
　Till one shall reach death's goal.'
Her burning tears blistered his heart ;
　Her pity flayed his soul.

' Sweetheart,' she pled, ' we can unite
　Life's torn and ravelled weft;
We yet may know love's deep delight :
　I have some beauty left.'

' But I am old—half dead ; alack !
　I know the double loss
Of song and love !' He warned her back,
　And broke his harp across.

E

She stretched her arms : her pleading eyes,
  Her pleading blush were vain;
He fled towards the sunset skies
  Across the shadowed plain.

For years he wandered far and near,
  And begged in silence sad;
The children shrank from him in fear ;
  The people called him mad.

Upon a ruddy ember eve
  They feasted in the hall :
The old broken man, with no one's leave,
  Sat down among them all.

And while the swarthy rafters rang
  With antique praise of wine,
There rose a conscious youth and sang
  A ditty new and fine.

Of Fate's mills, and the human grist
    They grind at, was his song ;
He cursed the canting moralist
    Who measures right and wrong.

' The earth, a flying tumour, wends
    Through space all blotched and blown
With suns and worlds, with odds and ends
    Of systems seamed and sewn :

' Beneath the sun it froths like yeast ;
    Its fiery essence flares ;
It festers into man and beast ;
    It throbs with flowers and tares.

' Behold ! 'tis but a heap of dust,
    Kneaded by fire and flood ;
While hunger fierce, and fiercer lust,
    Drench it with tears and blood.

'Yet why seek after some new birth ?
　　For surely, late or soon,
　This ague-fit we call the earth
　　Shall be a corpse-cold moon.

'Why need we, lacking help and hope,
　　By fears and fancies tossed,
　Vainly debate with ruthless Fate,
　　Fighting a battle lost ?

'Fill high the bowl !　We are the scum
　　Of matter ; fill the bowl ;
　Drink scathe to him, and death to him,
　　Who dreams he has a soul.'

　They clinked their cans and roared applause ;
　　The singer swelled with pride.
'You sneer and carp !　Give me the harp,'
　　The old man, trembling, cried.

They laughed and wondered, and grew still,
  To see one so aghast
Smiting the chords ; but all his skill
  Came back to him at last.

And lo, as searching-sweet as musk
  The words were and the tune,
The while he sang of dawn and dusk,
  Of midnight and of noon ;

Of heaven and hell, of times and tides ;
  Of wintry winds that blow,
Of spring that haunts the world and hides
  Her flowers among the snow ;

Of summer, rustling green and glad,
  With blossoms purfled fair ;
Of autumn's wine-stained mouth and sad,
  Wan eyes, and golden hair ;

Of Love, of Love, the wild sweet scent
  Of flowers, and words, and lives,
And loyal Nature's urgent bent
  Whereby the world survives ;

Of magic Love that opes the ports
  Of sense and soul, that saith
The moonlight's meaning, and extorts
  The fealty of Death.

He sang of peace and work that bless
  The simple and the sage ;
He sang of hope and happiness,
  He sang the Golden Age.

And the shamed listeners knew the spell
  That still enchants the years,
When the world's commonplaces fell
  In music on their ears.

'Go, bring a wreath of glossy bay
    To place upon his head !
A poet born !'   Woe worth the day,
    They crowned a poet dead !

Dead, while upon the pulsing string
    Still beat his early rhyme—
The song the poet born shall sing
    Until the end of Time !

SERENADE

(1250 A.D.)

WITH stars, with trailing galaxies,
    Like a white-rose bower in bloom,
Darkness garlands the vaulted skies,
    Day's adorn'd tomb ;
A whisper without from the briny west
    Thrills and sweetens the gloom ;
Within, Miranda seeks her rest
    High in her turret-room.

Armies upon her walls encamp
    In silk and silver thread ;
Chased and fretted, her silver lamp
    Dimly lights her bed ;

And now the silken screen is drawn,

    The velvet coverlet spread ;

And the pillow of down and snowy lawn

    Mantles about her head.

With violet-scented rain

    Sprinkle the rushy floor ;

Let the tapestry hide the tinted pane,

    And cover the chamber door ;

But leave a glimmering beam,

    Miranda belamour,

To touch and gild my waking dream,

    For I am your troubadour.

I sound my throbbing lyre,

    And sing to myself below ;

Her damsel sits beside the fire

    Crooning a song I know ;

The tapestry shakes on the wall,

    The shadows hurry and go,

The silent flames leap up and fall,

    And the muttering birch-logs glow.

Deep and sweet she sleeps,

    Because of her love for me ;

And deep and sweet the peace that keeps

    My happy heart in fee !

Peace on the heights, in the deeps,

    Peace over hill and lea,

Peace through the starlit steeps,

    Peace on the starlit sea,

Because a simple maiden sleeps

    Dreaming a dream of me !

A FROSTY MORNING

From heaven's high embrasure
   The sun with tufted rays
Illum'd the wandering azure
   And all the world's wide ways.

Usurping in its olden
   Abode the fog's demesne,
In watchet weeds and golden
   The still air sparkled keen.

On window-sill and door-post,
   On rail and tramway rust,
Embroidery of hoar-frost
   Was sewn like diamond dust.

Unthronged, or crowded densely
By people business-led,
The pavements, tuned intensely,
Rang hollow to the tread.

The traffic hurled and hammered
Down every ringing street ;
Like gongs the causeys clamoured,
Like drums the asphalt beat.

While ruling o'er the olden
Abode of fog unclean,
In watchet weeds and golden
The still air sparkled keen.

A BALLAD OF A WORKMAN

ALL day beneath polluted skies
    He laboured in a clanging town;
At night he read with bloodshot eyes
    And fondly dreamt of high renown.

' My time is filched by toil and sleep ;
    ' My heart,' he thought, 'is clogged with dust;
My soul that flashed from out the deep,
    A magic blade, begins to rust.

' For me the lamps of heaven shine ;
    For me the cunning seasons care ;
The old undaunted sea is mine,
    The stable earth, the ample air.

'Yet a dark street—at either end,

    A bed, an anvil—prisons me,

  Until my desperate state shall mend,

    And Death, the Saviour, set me free.

'Better a hundred times to die,

    And sink at once into the mould,

Than like a stagnant puddle lie

    With arabesques of scum enscrolled.

'I must go forth and view the sphere

    I own. What can my courage daunt?

Instead of dying daily here,

    The worst is dying once of want.

'I drop the dream of high renown;

    I ask but to possess my soul.'

At dawn he left the silent town,

    And quaking toward the forest stole.

He feared that he might want the wit

    To light on Nature's hidden hearth,

And deemed his rusty soul unfit

    To win the beauty of the earth.

But when he came among the trees,

    So slowly built, so many-ring'd,

His doubting thought could soar at ease

    In colour steep'd, with passion wing'd.

Occult remembrances awoke

    Of outlaws in the good greenwood,

And antique times of woaded folk

    Began to haunt his brain and blood.

No longer hope appeared a crime :

    He sang; his very heart and flesh

Aspired to join the ends of time,

    And forge and mould the world afresh.

' I dare not choose to run in vain;

 I must continue toward the goal.'

The pulse of life beat strong again,

 And in a flash he found his soul.

'The worker never knows defeat,

 Though unvictorious he may die :

The anvil and the grimy street,

 My destined throne and Calvary !'

Back to the town he hastened, bent—

 So swiftly did his passion change—

On selfless plans. 'I shall invent

 A means to amplify the range

'Of human power : find the soul wings,

 If not the body ! Let me give

Mankind more mastery over things,

 More thought, more joy, more will to live.'

He overtook upon the way

    A tottering ancient travel-worn :

'Lend me your arm, good youth, I pray;

    I scarce shall see another morn.'

Dread thought had carved his pallid face,

    And bowed his form, and blanched his hair;

In every part he bore some trace,

    Or some deep dint of uncouth care.

The workman led him to his room,

    And would have nursed him.   'No,' he said;

'It is my self-appointed doom

    To die upon a borrowed bed;

'But hear and note my slightest word.

    I am a man without a name.

I saw the Bastille fall; I heard

    The giant Mirabeau declaim.

F

' I saw the stormy dawn look pale

    Across the sea-bound battle-field,

  When through the hissing sleet and hail

    The clarions of Cromwell pealed :

' I watched the deep-souled Puritan

    Grow greater with the desperate strife :

  The cannon waked; the shouting van

    Charged home; and victory leapt to life.

' At Seville in the Royal square

    I saw Columbus as he passed

  Laurelled to greet the Catholic pair

    Who had believed in him at last :

' I saw the Andalusians fill

    Windows, and roofs, and balconies—

  A firmament of faces still,

    A galaxy of wondering eyes :

'For he had found the unknown shore,

    And made the world's great dream come true:

I think that men shall never more

    Know anything so strange and new.

'By meteor light when day had set

    I looked across Angora's plain,

And watched the fall of Bajazet,

    The victory of Tamerlane.

'In that old city where the vine

    Dislodged the seaweed, once I saw

The inexorable Florentine :

    He looked my way ; I bent with awe

'Before his glance, for this was he

    Who drained the dregs of sorrow's cup

In fierce disdain ; it seemed to me

    A spirit passed, my hair stood up.

' Draw nearer : breath and sight begin

　To fail me : nearer, ere I die.—

I saw the brilliant Saladin,

　Who taught the Christians courtesy;

' And Charlemagne, whose dreaded name,

　I first in far Bokhara heard;

Mohammed, with the eyes of flame,

　The lightning-blow, the thunder-word.

' I saw Him nailed upon a tree,

　Whom once beside an inland lake

I had beheld in Galilee

　Speaking as no man ever spake.

' I saw imperial Caesar fall;

　I saw the star of Macedon;

I saw from Troy's enchanted wall

　The death of Priam's mighty son.

'I heard in streets of Troy at night

    Cassandra prophesying fire. . . .

  A flamelit face upon my sight

    Flashes : I see the World's Desire !

'My life ebbs fast : nearer ! I sought

    A means to overmaster fate :

  Me, the Egyptian Hermes taught

    In old Hermopolis the Great :

'I pierced to Nature's inmost hearth,

    And wrung from her with toil untold

  The soul and substance of the earth,

    The seed of life, the seed of gold.

'Until the end I meant to stay;

    But thought has here so small a range;

  And I am tired of night and day,

    And tired of men who never change.

'All earthly hope ceased long ago;

   Yet, like a mother young and fond

Whose child is dead, I ache to know

   If there be anything beyond.

'Dark—all is darkness! Are you there?

   Give me your hand.—I choose to die.

This holds my secret—should you dare;

   And this, to bury me. . . . Good-bye.'

Amazement held the workman's soul;

   He took the alchemist's bequest—

A light purse and a parchment scroll;

   And watched him slowly sink to rest.

And nothing could he dream or think;

   He went like one bereft of sense,

Till passion overbore the brink

   Of all his wistful continence,

When his strange guest was laid in earth
 And he had read the scroll : 'Behold,
I can procure from Nature's hearth
 The Seed of Life, the Seed of Gold !

'For ever young ! Now, time and tide
 Must wait for me ; my life shall vie
With fate and fortune stride for stride
 Until the sun drops from the sky.

'Gold at a touch ! Nations and kings
 Shall come and go at my command ;
I shall control the secret springs
 Of enterprise in every land ;

'And hasten on the Perfect Day :
 Great men may break the galling chains ;
Sweet looks light up the toilsome way ;
 But I alone shall hold the reins !

' All fragrance, all delightfulness,

    And all the glory, all the power,

  That sound and colour can express,

    Shall be my ever-growing dower.

' And I shall know, and I shall love

    In every age, in every clime

  All beauty. . . . I, enthroned above

    Humanity, the peer of Time !

' Nay—selfish !   I shall give to men

    The Seed of Life, the seed of Gold ;

  Restore the Golden Age again

    At once, and let no soul grow old.

' But gold were then of no avail,

    And death would cease—unhallowed doom !

  The heady wine of life grow stale,

    And earth become a living tomb !

' And youth would end, and truth decline,

    And only pale illusion rule ;

For it is death makes love divine,

    Men human, life so sweet and full ! '

He burnt the scroll. ' I shall not cheat

    My destiny. Life, death for me !

The anvil and the grimy street,

    My unknown throne and Calvary !

' Only obedience can be great ;

    It brings the Golden Age again :

Even to be still, abiding fate,

    Is kingly ministry to men !

' I drop the dream of high renown :

    A nameless private in the strife,

Life, take me ; take me, clanging town ;

    And death, the eager zest of life.

'The hammered anvils reel and chime ;

   The breathless, belted wheels ring true ;

The workmen join the ends of time,

   And forge and mould the world anew.'

PIPER, PLAY !

Now the furnaces are out,
  And the aching anvils sleep ;
Down the road the grimy rout
  Tramples homeward twenty deep.
    Piper, play ! Piper, play !
      Though we be o'erlaboured men,
    Ripe for rest, pipe your best !
    Let us foot it once again !

Bridled looms delay their din ;
  All the humming wheels are spent ;
Busy spindles cease to spin ;
  Warp and woof must rest content.

Piper, play !   Piper, play !

For a little we are free !

Foot it girls and shake your curls,

Haggard creatures though we be !

Racked and soiled the faded air

Freshens in our holiday ;

Clouds and tides our respite share;

Breezes linger by the way.

Piper, rest !   Piper, rest !

Now, a carol of the moon !

Piper, piper, play your best !

Melt the sun into your tune !

We are of the humblest grade ;

Yet we dare to dance our fill :

Male and female were we made—

Fathers, mothers, lovers still !

Piper—softly ; soft and low ;

    Pipe of love in mellow notes,

Till the tears begin to flow,

    And our hearts are in our throats !

Nameless as the stars of night

    Far in galaxies unfurled,

Yet we wield unrivalled might,

    Joints and hinges of the world !

      Night and day ! night and day !

        Sound the song the hours rehearse !

      Work and play ! work and play !

        The order of the universe !

Now the furnaces are out,

    And the aching anvils sleep ;

Down the road a merry rout

    Dances homeward, twenty deep.

Piper, play ! Piper, play !

Wearied people though we be,

Ripe for rest, pipe your best !

For a little we are free !

A NEW BALLAD OF TANNHÄUSER*

'WHAT hardy, tattered wretch is that
    Who on our Synod dares intrude?'
Pope Urban with his council sat,
    And near the door Tannhäuser stood.

His eye with light unearthly gleamed;
    His yellow hair hung round his head
In elf locks lusterless: he seemed
    Like one new-risen from the dead.

'Hear me, most Holy Father, tell
    The tale that burns my soul within.
I stagger on the brink of hell;
    No voice but yours can shrive my sin.'

* See note at the end of the book.

' Speak, sinner.'　' From my father's house
　　Lightly I stepped in haste for fame ;
　And hoped by deeds adventurous
　　High on the world to carve my name.

' At early dawn I took my way,
　　My heart with peals of gladness rang ;
　Nor could I leave the woods all day,
　　Because the birds so sweetly sang.

' But when the happy birds had gone
　　To rest, and night with panic fears
　And blushes deep came stealing on,
　　Another music thrilled my ears.

' I heard the evening wind serene,
　　And all the wandering waters sing
　The deep delight the day had been,
　　The deep delight the night would bring.

' I heard the wayward earth express

    In one long-drawn melodious sigh

The rapture of the sun's caress,

    The passion of the brooding sky.

' The air, a harp of myriad chords,

    Intently murmured overhead;

My heart grew great with unsung words:

    I followed where the music led.

' It led me to a mountain-chain,

    Wherein athwart the deepening gloom,

High-hung above the wooded plain,

    Appeared a summit like a tomb.

' Aloft a giddy pathway wound

    That brought me to a darksome cave :

I heard, undaunted, underground

    Wild winds and wilder voices rave,

                G

' And plunged into that stormy world.

    Cold hands assailed me impotent

   In the gross darkness; serpents curled

    About my limbs; but on I went.

' The wild winds buffeted my face;

    The wilder voices shrieked despair;

   A stealthy step with mine kept pace,

    And subtle terror steeped the air.

' But the sweet sound that throbbed on high

    Had left the upper world; and still

   A cry rang in my heart—a cry !

    For lo, far in the hollow hill,

' The dulcet melody withdrawn

    Kept welling through the fierce uproar.

   As I have seen the molten dawn

    Across a swarthy tempest pour,

'So suddenly the magic note,

  Transformed to light, a glittering brand,

Out of the storm and darkness smote

  A peaceful sky, a dewy land.

'I scarce could breathe, I might not stir,

  The while there came across the lea,

With singing maidens after her,

  A woman wonderful to see.

'Her face—her face was strong and sweet;

  Her looks were loving prophecies;

She kissed my brow : I kissed her feet—

  A woman wonderful to kiss.

'She took me to a place apart

  Where eglantine and roses wove

A bower, and gave me all her heart—

  A woman wonderful to love.

' As I lay worshipping my bride,

　　While rose leaves in her bosom fell,

　And dreams came sailing on a tide

　　Of sleep, I heard a matin bell.

' It beat my soul as with a rod

　　Tingling with horror of my sin ;

　I thought of Christ, I thought of God,

　　And of the fame I meant to win.

' I rose ; I ran ; nor looked behind ;

　　The doleful voices shrieked despair

　In tones that pierced the crashing wind ;

　　And subtle terror warped the air.

' About my limbs the serpents curled;

　　The stealthy step with mine kept pace;

　But soon I reached the upper world :

　　I sought a priest; I prayed for grace.

' He said, " Sad sinner, do you know

   What fiend this is, the baleful cause

 Of your dismay?"   I loved her so

   I never asked her what she was.

' He said, " Perhaps not God above

   Can pardon such unheard-of ill:

 It was the pagan Queen of Love

   Who lured you to her haunted hill!

' " Each hour you spent with her was more

   Than a full year?   Only the Pope

 Can tell what heaven may have in store

   For one who seems past help and hope."

' Forthwith I took the way to Rome :

   I scarcely slept; I scarcely ate :

 And hither quaking am I come,

   But resolute to know my fate.

'Most Holy Father, save my soul ! . . .

   Ah God ! again I hear the chime,

Sweeter than liquid bells that toll

   Across a lake at vesper time . . .

'Her eyelids drop . . . I hear her sigh . . .

   The roseleaves fall. . . . She falls asleep .ı. .

The cry rings in my blood—the cry

   That surges from the deepest deep.

'No man was ever tempted so !—

   I say not this in my defence. . . .

Help, Father, help ! or I must go !

   The dulcet music draws me hence !'

He knelt—he fell upon his face.

   Pope Urban said, ' The eternal cost

Of guilt like yours eternal grace

   Dare not remit : your soul is lost.

' When this dead staff I carry grows

    Again and blossoms, heavenly light

May shine on you.'   Tannhäuser rose ;

    And all at once his face grew bright.

He saw the emerald leaves unfold,

    The emerald blossoms break and glance ;

They watched him, wondering to behold

    The rapture of his countenance.

The undivined, eternal God

    Looked on him from the highest heaven,

And showed him by the budding rod

    There was no need to be forgiven.

He heard melodious voices call

    Across the world, an elfin shout ;

And when he left the council-hall,   ·

    It seemed a great light had gone out.

With anxious heart, with troubled brow,
　　The Synod turned upon the Pope.
They saw; they cried, 'A living bough,
　　A miracle, a pledge of hope!'

And Urban trembling saw: 'God's way
　　Is not as man's,' he said. 'Alack!
Forgive me, gracious heaven, this day
　　My sin of pride. Go, bring him back.'

But swift as thought Tannhäuser fled,
　　And was not found. He scarcely slept;
He scarcely ate; for overhead
　　The ceaseless, dulcet music kept

Wafting him on. And evermore
　　The foliate staff he saw at Rome
Pointed the way; and the winds bore
　　Sweet voices whispering him to come.

The air, a world-enfolding flood

    Of liquid music poured along ;

And the wild cry within his blood

    Became at last a golden song.

' All day,' he sang—' I feel all day

    The earth dilate beneath my feet ;

I hear in fancy far away

    The tidal heart of ocean beat.

' My heart amasses as I run

    The depth of heaven's sapphire flower ;

The resolute, enduring sun

    Fulfils my soul with splendid power.

' I quiver with divine desire;

    I clasp the stars; my thoughts immerse

Themselves in space; like fire in fire

    I melt into the universe.

'For I am running to my love :

 The eager roses burn below ;

Orion wheels his sword above,

 To guard the way God bids me go.'

At dusk he reached the mountain chain,

 Wherein athwart the deepening gloom,

High hung above the wooded plain

 The Hörselberg rose like a tomb.

He plunged into the under-world;

 Cold hands assailed him impotent

In the gross darkness; serpents curled

 About his limbs ; but on he went.

The wild winds buffeted his face ;

 The wilder voices shrieked despair ;

A stealthy step with his kept pace ;

 And subtle terror steeped the air.

But once again the magic note,

    Transformed to light, a glittering brand,

Out of the storm and darkness smote

    A peaceful sky, a dewy land.

And once again he might not stir,

    The while there came across the lea

With singing maidens after her

    The Queen of Love so fair to see.

Her happy face was strong and sweet ;

    Her looks were loving prophecies ;

She kissed his brow ; he kissed her feet—

    He kissed the ground her feet did kiss.

She took him to a place apart

    Where eglantine and roses wove

A bower, and gave him all her heart—

    The Queen of Love, the Queen of Love.

As he lay worshipping his bride
  While rose-leaves in her bosom fell,
And dreams came sailing on a tide
  Of sleep, he heard a matin-bell.

'Hark! Let us leave the magic hill,'
  He said, 'And live on earth with men.'
'No; here,' she said, 'we stay, until
  The Golden Age shall come again.'

And so they wait, while empires sprung
  Of hatred thunder past above,
Deep in the earth for ever young
  Tannhäuser and the Queen of Love.

His heart was worn and sore ;
He was old before his time ;
He had wasted half his life.

Night—it was always night,
And never a star above :
But the ring of a manly stroke,
The flash of a gentle look,
The touch of a comrade's hand
Groping for his on the march,
Were more to him than the day.

At the thought of his youth,

At the pulse of love,

At the swoop of death,

He sang aloud in the dark,

And touched the heart of the world.

NOTE

THE story of Tannhäuser is best known in the sophisticated version of Wagner's great opera. In reverting to a simpler form I have endeavoured to present passion rather than sentiment, and once more to bear a hand in laying the ghost of an unwholesome idea that still haunts the world—the idea of the inherent impurity of nature.

I beg to submit to those who may be disposed to think with me, and also to those who, although otherwise minded, are at liberty to alter their opinions, that ' A New Ballad of Tannhäuser' is not only the most modern, but the most humane interpretation of the world-legend with which it deals.

J. D.

JOHN LANE

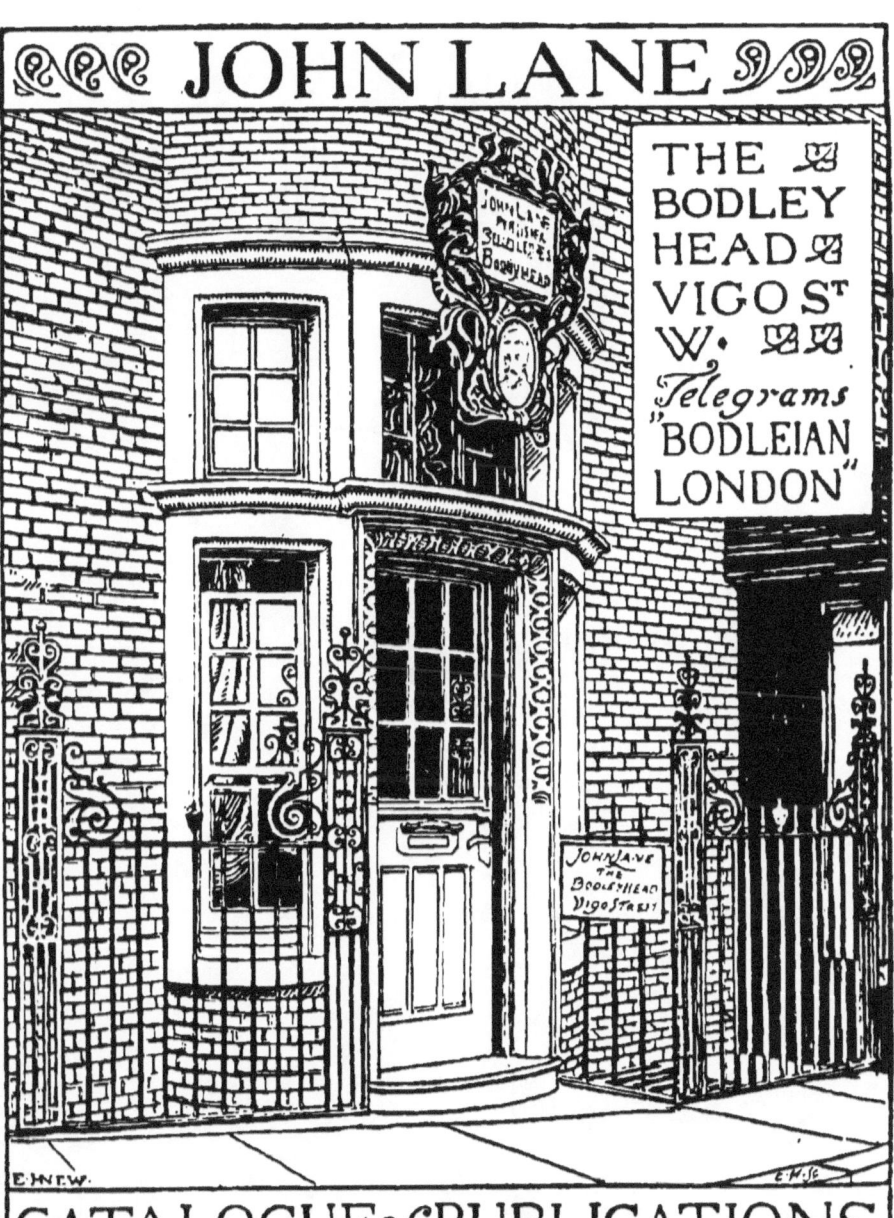

THE BODLEY HEAD VIGO St W. Telegrams "BODLEIAN LONDON"

JOHN LANE THE BODLEY HEAD VIGO STREET

CATALOGUE of PUBLICATIONS in BELLES LETTRES all at net prices

List of Books

IN

BELLES LETTRES

Published by John Lane

The Bodley Head

VIGO STREET, LONDON, W.

Adams (Francis).
ESSAYS IN MODERNITY. Crown 8vo.
5s. net. [*Shortly.*
A CHILD OF THE AGE. (*See* KEY-
NOTES SERIES.)

A. E.
HOMEWARD SONGS BY THE WAY.
Sq. 16mo, wrappers. 1s. 6d. net.
*Transferred to the present Pub-
lisher.* [*Second Edition.*

Aldrich (T. B.)
LATER LYRICS. Sm. Fcap. 8vo.
2s. 6d. net.

Allen (Grant).
THE LOWER SLOPES: A Volume of
Verse. With Title-page and Cover
Design by J. ILLINGWORTH KAY.
Crown 8vo. 5s. net.
THE WOMAN WHO DID. (*See* KEY-
NOTES SERIES.)
THE BRITISH BARBARIANS. (*See*
KEYNOTES SERIES.)

Arcady Library (The).
A Series of Open-Air Books. Edited
by J. S. FLETCHER. With Cover
Designs by PATTEN WILSON.
Each volume crown 8vo. 5s. net.
   I. ROUND ABOUT A BRIGHTON
     COACH OFFICE. By MAUDE
     EGERTON KING. With
     over 30 Illustrations by
     LUCY KEMP-WELCH.
   II. LIFE IN ARCADIA. By J. S.
     FLETCHER. Illustrated by
     PATTEN WILSON.

Arcady Library (The)—*cont.*
   III. SCHOLAR GIPSIES. By JOHN
     BUCHAN. With 7 full-page
     Etchings by D.Y. CAMERON
The following is in preparation :
   IV. IN THE GARDEN OF PEACE.
     By HELEN MILMAN. With
     Illustrations by EDMUND
     H. NEW.

Beeching (Rev. H. C.).
IN A GARDEN : Poems. With Title-
page designed by ROGER FRY.
Crown 8vo. 5s. net.
ST. AUGUSTINE AT OSTIA. Crown
8vo, wrappers. 1s. net.

Beerbohm (Max).
THE WORKS OF MAX BEERBOHM.
With a Bibliography by JOHN
LANE. Sq. 16mo. 4s. 6d. net.

Benson (Arthur Christopher)
LYRICS. Fcap. 8vo, buckram. 5s.
net.
LORD VYET AND OTHER POEMS.
Fcap. 8vo. 3s. 6d. net.

**Bodley Head Anthologies
(The).**
Edited by ROBERT H. CASE. With
Title-page and Cover Designs by
WALTER WEST. Each volume
crown 8vo. 5s. net.
   I. ENGLISH EPITHALAMIES.
     By ROBERT H. CASE.

Bodley Head Anthologies (The)—*continued.*

II. MUSA PISCATRIX. By JOHN BUCHAN. With 6 Etchings by E. PHILIP PIMLOTT.

III. ENGLISH ELEGIES. By JOHN C BAILEY.

IV. ENGLISH SATIRES. By CHAS. HILL DICK.

Bridges (Robert).

SUPPRESSED CHAPTERS AND OTHER BOOKISHNESS. Crown 8vo. 3s. 6d. net. [*Second Edition.*

Brotherton (Mary).

ROSEMARY FOR REMEMBRANCE. With Title-page and Cover Design by WALTER WEST. Fcap. 8vo. 3s. 6d. net.

Crackanthorpe (Hubert).

VIGNETTES. A Miniature Journal of Whim and Sentiment. Fcap. 8vo, boards. 2s. 6d. net.

Crane (Walter).

TOY BOOKS. Re-issue, each with new Cover Design and End Papers. This LITTLE PIG'S PICTURE BOOK, containing:

I. THIS LITTLE PIG.

II. THE FAIRY SHIP.

III. KING LUCKIEBOY'S PARTY.

The three bound in one volume with a decorative cloth cover, end papers, and a newly written and designed preface and title-page. 3s. 6d. net; separately 9d. net each.

MOTHER HUBBARD'S PICTURE BOOK, containing:

I. MOTHER HUBBARD'S.

II. THE THREE BEARS.

III. THE ABSURD A. B. C.

The three bound in one volume with a decorative cloth cover, end papers, and a newly written and designed preface and title-page. 3s. 6d. net; separately 9d. net each.

Custance (Olive).

FIRST FRUITS: Poems. Fcap. 8vo. 3s. 6d. net.

Dalmon (C. W.).

SONG FAVOURS. With a Title-page by J. P. DONNE. Sq. 16mo. 3s. 6d. net.

Davidson (John).

PLAYS: An Unhistorical Pastoral; A Romantic Farce; Bruce, a Chronicle Play; Smith, a Tragic Farce; Scaramouch in Naxos, a Pantomime. With a Frontispiece and Cover Design by AUBREY BEARDSLEY. Small 4to. 7s. 6d. net.

FLEET STREET ECLOGUES. Fcap. 8vo, buckram. 4s. 6d. net. [*Third Edition.*

FLEET STREET ECLOGUES. 2nd Series. Fcap. 8vo, buckram. 4s. 6d. net. [*Second Edition.*

A RANDOM ITINERARY AND A BALLAD. With a Frontispiece and Title-page by LAURENCE HOUSMAN. Fcap. 8vo, Irish Linen. 5s. net.

BALLADS AND SONGS. With a Title-page and Cover Design by WALTER WEST. Fcap. 8vo, buckram. 5s. net. [*Fourth Edition.*

NEW BALLADS. Fcap. 8vo, buckram. 4s. 6d. net.

De Tabley (Lord)

POEMS, DRAMATIC AND LYRICAL. By JOHN LEICESTER WARREN (Lord de Tabley). Illustrations and Cover Design by C. S. RICKETTS. Crown 8vo. 7s. 6d. net. [*Third Edition.*

POEMS, DRAMATIC AND LYRICAL. Second Series, uniform in binding with the former volume. Crown 8vo. 5s. net.

Duer (Caroline, and Alice).

POEMS. Fcap. 8vo. 3s. 6d. net.

Egerton (George)

KEYNOTES. (*See* KEYNOTES SERIES.)

DISCORDS. (*See* KEYNOTES SERIES.)

YOUNG OFEG'S DITTIES. A translation from the Swedish of OLA HANSSON. With Title-page and Cover Design by AUBREY BEARDSLEY. Crown 8vo. 3s. 6d. net.

SYMPHONIES. [*In preparation.*

Eglinton (John).

TWO ESSAYS ON THE REMNANT. Post 8vo, wrappers. 1s. 6d. net. *Transferred to the present Publisher.* [*Second Edition.*

Eve's Library.

Each volume, crown 8vo. 3s. 6d. net.

I. MODERN WOMEN. An English rendering of LAURA MARHOLM HANSSON'S "DAS BUCH DER FRAUEN" by HERMIONE RAMSDEN. Subjects: Sonia Kovalevsky, George Egerton, Eleanora Duse, Amalie Skram, Marie Bashkirtseff, A. Ch. Edgren Leffler.

II. THE ASCENT OF WOMAN. By ROY DEVEREUX.

III. MARRIAGE QUESTIONS IN MODERN FICTION. By ELIZABETH RACHEL CHAPMAN.

Fea (Allan).

THE FLIGHT OF THE KING: a full, true, and particular account of the escape of His Most Sacred Majesty King Charles II. after the Battle of Worcester, with Twelve Portraits in Photogravure and nearly 100 other Illustrations. Demy 8vo. 21s. net.

Field (Eugene).

THE LOVE AFFAIRS OF A BIBLIOMANIAC. Post 8vo. 3s. 6d. net.

Fletcher (J. S.).

THE WONDERFUL WAPENTAKE. By "A SON OF THE SOIL." With 18 full-page Illustrations by J. A. SYMINGTON. Crown 8vo. 5s. 6d. net.

LIFE IN ARCADIA. (*See* ARCADY LIBRARY.)

GOD'S FAILURES. (*See* KEYNOTES SERIES.)

BALLADS OF REVOLT. Sq. 32mo. 2s. 6d. net.

Ford (James L.).

THE LITERARY SHOP AND OTHER TALES. Fcap. 8vo. 3s. 6d. net.

Four-and-Sixpenny Novels

Each volume with Title-page and Cover Design by PATTEN WILSON. Crown 8vo. 4s. 6d. net.

GALLOPING DICK. By H. B. MARRIOTT WATSON.

THE WOOD OF THE BRAMBLES. By FRANK MATHEW.

THE SACRIFICE OF FOOLS. By R. MANIFOLD CRAIG.

A LAWYER'S WIFE. By Sir NEVILL GEARY, Bart. [*Second Edition.*

The following are in preparation :

WEIGHED IN THE BALANCE. By HARRY LANDER.

GLAMOUR. By META ORRED.

PATIENCE SPARHAWK AND HER TIMES. By GERTRUDE ATHERTON.

THE WISE AND THE WAYWARD. By G. S. STREET.

MIDDLE GREYNESS. By A. J. DAWSON.

THE MARTYR'S BIBLE. By GEORGE FIFTH.

A CELIBATE'S WIFE. By HERBERT FLOWERDEW.

MAX. By JULIAN CROSKEY.

Fuller (H. B.).

THE PUPPET BOOTH. Twelve Plays. Crown 8vo. 4s. 6d. net.

Gale (Norman).

ORCHARD SONGS. With Title-page and Cover Design by J. ILLINGWORTH KAY. Fcap. 8vo, Irish Linen. 5s. net.

Also a Special Edition limited in number on hand-made paper bound in English vellum. £1 1s. net.

Garnett (Richard).

POEMS. With Title-page by J. ILLINGWORTH KAY. Crown 8vo. 5s. net.

DANTE, PETRARCH, CAMOENS, cxxiv Sonnets, rendered in English. With Title-page by PATTEN WILSON. Crown 8vo. 5s. net.

Gibson (Charles Dana).

PICTURES : Eighty-Five Large Cartoons. Oblong Folio. 15s. net.

PICTURES OF PEOPLE. Eighty-Five Large Cartoons. Oblong folio. 15s. net.

[*In preparation.*

Gosse (Edmund).

THE LETTERS OF THOMAS LOVELL BEDDOES. Now first edited. Pott 8vo. 5s. net.

Also 25 copies large paper. 12s. 6d. net.

Grahame (Kenneth).

PAGAN PAPERS. With Title-page by AUBREY BEARDSLEY. Fcap. 8vo. 5s. net.

[Out of Print at present.

THE GOLDEN AGE. With Cover Design by CHARLES ROBINSON. Crown 8vo. 3s. 6d. net.

[Fifth Edition.

Greene (G. A.).

ITALIAN LYRISTS OF TO-DAY. Translations in the original metres from about thirty-five living Italian poets, with bibliographical and biographical notes. Crown 8vo. 5s. net.

Greenwood (Frederick).

IMAGINATION IN DREAMS. Crown 8vo. 5s. net.

Hake (T. Gordon).

A SELECTION FROM HIS POEMS. Edited by Mrs. MEYNELL. With a Portrait after D. G. ROSSETTI, and a Cover Design by GLEESON WHITE. Crown 8vo. 5s. net.

Hayes (Alfred).

THE VALE OF ARDEN AND OTHER POEMS. With a Title-page and a Cover designed by E. H. NEW. Fcap. 8vo. 3s. 6d. net.

Also 25 copies large paper. 15s. net.

Hazlitt (William).

LIBER AMORIS; OR, THE NEW PYGMALION. Edited, with an Introduction, by RICHARD LE GALLIENNE. To which is added an exact transcript of the original MS., Mrs. Hazlitt's Diary in Scotland, and letters never before published. Portrait after BEWICK, and facsimile letters. 400 Copies only. 4to, 364 pp., buckram. 21s. net.

Heinemann (William).

THE FIRST STEP; A Dramatic Moment. Small 4to. 3s. 6d. net.

Hopper (Nora).

BALLADS IN PROSE. With a Title-page and Cover by WALTER WEST. Sq. 16mo. 5s. net.

UNDER QUICKEN BOUGHS. With Title-page designed by PATTEN WILSON, and Cover designed by ELIZABETH NAYLOR. Crown 8vo. 5s. net.

Housman (Clemence).

THE WERE WOLF. With 6 full-page Illustrations, Title-page, and Cover Design by LAURENCE HOUSMAN. Sq. 16mo. 3s. 6d. net.

Housman (Laurence).

GREEN ARRAS: Poems. With 6 Illustrations, Title-page, Cover Design, and End Papers by the Author. Crown 8vo. 5s. net.

GODS AND THEIR MAKERS. Crown 8vo. 5s. net. [In preparation.

Irving (Laurence).

GODEFROI AND YOLANDE: A Play. Sm. 4to. 3s. 6d. net.

[In preparation.

James (W. P.)

ROMANTIC PROFESSIONS: A Volume of Essays. With Title-page designed by J. ILLINGWORTH KAY. Crown 8vo. 5s. net.

Johnson (Lionel).

THE ART OF THOMAS HARDY: Six Essays. With Etched Portrait by WM. STRANG, and Bibliography by JOHN LANE. Crown 8vo. 5s. 6d. net. [Second Edition.

Also 150 copies, large paper, with proofs of the portrait. £1 1s. net.

Johnson (Pauline).

WHITE WAMPUM: Poems. With a Title-page and Cover Design by E. H. NEW. Crown 8vo. 5s. net.

Johnstone (C. E.).

BALLADS OF BOY AND BEAK. With a Title-page by F. H. TOWNSEND. Sq. 32mo. 2s. net.

Keynotes Series.

Each volume with specially-designed Title-page by AUBREY BEARDS-LEY or PATTEN WILSON. Crown 8vo, cloth. 3s. 6d. net.

I. KEYNOTES. By GEORGE EGERTON.
[*Seventh Edition.*

II. THE DANCING FAUN. By FLORENCE FARR.

III. POOR FOLK. Translated from the Russian of F. Dostoievsky by LENA MILMAN. With a Preface by GEORGE MOORE.

IV. A CHILD OF THE AGE. By FRANCIS ADAMS.

V. THE GREAT GOD PAN AND THE INMOST LIGHT. By ARTHUR MACHEN.
[*Second Edition.*

VI. DISCORDS. By GEORGE EGERTON.
[*Fifth Edition.*

VII. PRINCE ZALESKI. By M. P. SHIEL.

VIII. THE WOMAN WHO DID. By GRANT ALLEN.
[*Twenty-second Edition.*

IX. WOMEN'S TRAGEDIES. By H. D. LOWRY.

X. GREY ROSES. By HENRY HARLAND.

XI. AT THE FIRST CORNER AND OTHER STORIES. By H. B. MARRIOTT WATSON.

XII. MONOCHROMES. By ELLA D'ARCY.

XIII. AT THE RELTON ARMS. By EVELYN SHARP.

XIV. THE GIRL FROM THE FARM. By GERTRUDE DIX.
[*Second Edition.*

XV. THE MIRROR OF MUSIC. By STANLEY V. MAKOWER.

XVI. YELLOW AND WHITE. By W. CARLTON DAWE.

XVII. THE MOUNTAIN LOVERS. By FIONA MACLEOD.

XVIII. THE WOMAN WHO DIDN'T. By VICTORIA CROSSE.
[*Third Edition.*

Keynotes Series—*continued.*

XIX. THE THREE IMPOSTORS. By ARTHUR MACHEN.

XX. NOBODY'S FAULT. By NETTA SYRETT.
[*Second Edition.*

XXI. THE BRITISH BARBARIANS. By GRANT ALLEN.
[*Second Edition.*

XXII. IN HOMESPUN. By E. NESBIT.

XXIII. PLATONIC AFFECTIONS. By JOHN SMITH.

XXIV. NETS FOR THE WIND. By UNA TAYLOR.

XXV. WHERE THE ATLANTIC MEETS THE LAND. By CALDWELL LIPSETT.

XXVI. IN SCARLET AND GREY. By FLORENCE HENNIKER. (With THE SPECTRE OF THE REAL by FLORENCE HENNIKER and THOMAS HARDY.) [*Second Edition.*

XXVII. MARIS STELLA. By MARIE CLOTHILDE BALFOUR.

XXVIII. DAY BOOKS. By MABEL E. WOTTON.

XXIX. SHAPES IN THE FIRE. By M. P. SHIEL.

XXX. UGLY IDOL. By CLAUD NICHOLSON.

The following are in rapid preparation:

XXXI. KAKEMONOS. By W. CARLTON DAWE.

XXXII. GOD'S FAILURES. By J. S. FLETCHER.

XXXIII. A DELIVERANCE. By ALLAN MONKHOUSE.

XXXIV. MERE SENTIMENT. By A. J. DAWSON.

Lane's Library.

Each volume crown 8vo. 3s. 6d. net.

I. MARCH HARES. By GEORGE FORTH.
[*Second Edition.*

II. THE SENTIMENTAL SEX. By GERTRUDE WARDEN.

III. GOLD. By ANNIE LINDEN.

Lane's Library—*continued.*

The following are in preparation:
IV. BROKEN AWAY. By BEA-
TRICE GRIMSHAW.
V. RICHARD LARCH. By E. A.
BENNETT.
VI. THE DUKE OF LINDEN. By
JOSEPH F. CHARLES.

Leather (R. K.).

VERSES. 250 copies. Fcap. 8vo.
3s. net. [*Transferred to the
present Publisher.*

Lefroy (Edward Cracroft.)

POEMS. With a Memoir by W. A.
GILL, and a reprint of Mr. J. A.
SYMONDS' Critical Essay on
"Echoes from Theocritus." Cr.
8vo. Photogravure Portrait. 5s.
net.

Le Gallienne (Richard).

PROSE FANCIES. With Portrait of
the Author by WILSON STEER.
Crown 8vo. Purple cloth. 5s.
net. [*Fourth Edition.*
Also a limited large paper edition.
12s. 6d. net.

THE BOOK BILLS OF NARCISSUS,
An Account rendered by RICHARD
LE GALLIENNE. With a Frontispiece. Crown 8vo, purple cloth.
3s. 6d. net. [*Third Edition.*
Also 50 copies on large paper. 8vo.
10s. 6d. net.

ROBERT LOUIS STEVENSON, AN
ELEGY, AND OTHER POEMS,
MAINLY PERSONAL. With Etched
Title-page by D. Y. CAMERON.
Crown 8vo, purple cloth. 4s. 6d.
net.
Also 75 copies on large paper. 8vo.
12s. 6d. net.

ENGLISH POEMS. Crown 8vo, purple cloth. 4s. 6d. net.
[*Fourth Edition, revised.*

GEORGE MEREDITH: Some Char-
acteristics. With a Bibliography
(much enlarged) by JOHN LANE,
portrait, &c. Crown 8vo, purple
cloth. 5s. 6d. net.
[*Fourth Edition.*

Le Gallienne (Richard)—*continued.*

THE RELIGION OF A LITERARY
MAN. Crown 8vo, purple cloth.
3s. 6d. net. [*Fifth Thousand.*
Also a special rubricated edition on
hand-made paper. 8vo. 10s. 6d. net.

RETROSPECTIVE REVIEWS, A LITER-
ARY LOG, 1891-1895. 2 vols.
Crown 8vo, purple cloth. 9s.
net.

PROSE FANCIES. (Second Series).
Crown 8vo, Purple cloth. 5s. net.

THE QUEST OF THE GOLDEN GIRL.
Crown 8vo. 5s. net.
[*In preparation.*
See also HAZLITT, WALTON and
COTTON.

Lowry (H. D.).

MAKE BELIEVE. Illustrated by
CHARLES ROBINSON. Crown 8vo,
gilt edges or uncut. 5s. net.

WOMEN'S TRAGEDIES. (*See* KEY-
NOTES SERIES).

Lucas (Winifred).

UNITS: Poems. Fcap. 8vo. 3s. 6d.
net.

Lynch (Hannah).

THE GREAT GALEOTO AND FOLLY
OR SAINTLINESS. Two Plays,
from the Spanish of JOSÉ ECHE-
GARAY, with an Introduction.
Small 4to. 5s. 6d. net.

Marzials (Theo.).

THE GALLERY OF PIGEONS AND
OTHER POEMS. Post 8vo. 4s. 6d.
net. [*Transferred to the present
Publisher.*

The Mayfair Set.

Each volume fcap. 8vo. 3s. 6d. net.
I. THE AUTOBIOGRAPHY OF A
BOY. Passages selected by
his friend G. S. STREET.
With a Title-page designed
by C. W. FURSE.
[*Fifth Edition.*
II. THE JONESES AND THE
ASTERISKS. A Story in
Monologue. By GERALD
CAMPBELL. With a Title-
page and 6 Illustrations by
F. H. TOWNSEND.
[*Second Edition.*

The Mayfair Set—*continued.*

III. SELECT CONVERSATIONS WITH AN UNCLE, NOW EXTINCT. By H. G. WELLS. With a Title-page by F. H. TOWNSEND.

IV. FOR PLAIN WOMEN ONLY. By GEORGE FLEMING. With a Title-page by PATTEN WILSON.

V. THE FEASTS OF AUTOLYCUS: THE DIARY OF A GREEDY WOMAN. Edited by ELIZABETH ROBINS PENNELL. With a Title-page by PATTEN WILSON.

VI. MRS. ALBERT GRUNDY: OBSERVATIONS IN PHILISTIA. By HAROLD FREDERIC. With a Title-page by PATTEN WILSON. [*Second Edition.*

Meredith (George).

THE FIRST PUBLISHED PORTRAIT OF THIS AUTHOR, engraved on the wood by W. BISCOMBE GARDNER, after the painting by G. F. WATTS. Proof copies on Japanese vellum, signed by painter and engraver. £1 1s. net.

Meynell (Mrs.).

POEMS. Fcap. 8vo. 3s. 6d. net. [*Fourth Edition.*

THE RHYTHM OF LIFE AND OTHER ESSAYS. Fcap. 8vo. 3s. 6d. net. [*Third Edition.*

THE COLOUR OF LIFE AND OTHER ESSAYS. Fcap. 8vo. 3s. 6d. net. [*Second Edition.*

THE DARLING YOUNG. Fcap. 8vo. 3s. 6d. net. [*In preparation.*

Miller (Joaquin).

THE BUILDING OF THE CITY BEAUTIFUL. Fcap. 8vo. With a Decorated Cover. 5s. net.

Money-Coutts (F. B.).

POEMS. With Title-page designed by PATTEN WILSON. Crown 8vo. 3s. 6d. net.

Monkhouse (Allan).

BOOKS AND PLAYS: A Volume of Essays on Meredith, Borrow, Ibsen, and others. Crown 8vo. 5s. net.

Nesbit (E.).

A POMANDER OF VERSE. With a Title-page and Cover designed by LAURENCE HOUSMAN. Crown 8vo. 5s. net.

IN HOMESPUN. (*See* KEYNOTES SERIES.)

Nettleship (J. T.).

ROBERT BROWNING: Essays and Thoughts. Crown 8vo. 5s. 6d. net. [*Third Edition.*

Noble (Jas. Ashcroft).

THE SONNET IN ENGLAND AND OTHER ESSAYS. Title-page and Cover Design by AUSTIN YOUNG. Crown 8vo. 5s. net.

Also 50 copies large paper 12s. 6d. net

Oppenheim (Michael).

A HISTORY OF THE ADMINISTRATION OF THE ROYAL NAVY, and of Merchant Shipping in relation to the Navy from MDIX to MDCLX, with an introduction treating of the earlier period. With Illustrations. Demy 8vo. 15s. net.

O'Shaughnessy (Arthur).

HIS LIFE AND HIS WORK. With Selections from his Poems. By LOUISE CHANDLER MOULTON. Portrait and Cover Design. Fcap. 8vo. 5s. net.

Oxford Characters.

A series of lithographed portraits by WILL ROTHENSTEIN, with text by F. YORK POWELL and others. 200 copies only, folio, buckram. £3 3s. net.

25 special large paper copies containing proof impressions of the portraits signed by the artist, £6 6s. net.

Peters (Wm. Theodore).

POSIES OUT OF RINGS. With Title-page by PATTEN WILSON. Sq. 16mo. 2s. 6d. net.

Pierrot's Library.
Each volume with Title-page, Cover and End Papers, designed by AUBREY BEARDSLEY. Sq. 16mo. 2s. net.

 I. PIERROT. By H. DE VERE STACPOOLE.
 II. MY LITTLE LADY ANNE. By Mrs. EGERTON CASTLE.
 III. SIMPLICITY. By A. T. G. PRICE.
 IV. MY BROTHER. By VINCENT BROWN.

The following are in preparation:

 V. DEATH, THE KNIGHT, AND THE LADY. By H. DE VERE STACPOOLE.
 VI. MR. PASSINGHAM. By THOMAS COBB.
 VII. TWO IN CAPTIVITY. By VINCENT BROWN.

Plarr (Victor).
IN THE DORIAN MOOD: Poems. With Title-page by PATTEN WILSON. Crown 8vo. 5s. net.

Radford (Dollie).
SONGS AND OTHER VERSES. With a Title-page by PATTEN WILSON. Fcap. 8vo. 4s. 6d. net.

Rhys (Ernest).
A LONDON ROSE AND OTHER RHYMES. With Title-page designed by SELWYN IMAGE. Crown 8vo. 5s. net.

Robertson (John M.).
ESSAYS TOWARDS A CRITICAL METHOD. (New Series.) Crown 8vo. 5s. net. [*In preparation.*

St. Cyres (Lord).
THE LITTLE FLOWERS OF ST. FRANCIS: A new rendering into English of the Fioretti di San Francesco. Crown 8vo. 5s. net. [*In preparation.*

Seaman (Owen).
THE BATTLE OF THE BAYS. Fcap. 8vo. 3s. 6d. net.

Sedgwick (Jane Minot).
SONGS FROM THE GREEK. Fcap. 8vo. 3s. 6d. net.

Setoun (Gabriel).
THE CHILD WORLD: Poems. Illustrated by CHARLES ROBINSON. Crown 8vo. gilt edges or uncut. 5s. net. [*In preparation.*

Sharp (Evelyn).
WYMPS: Fairy Tales. With Coloured Illustrations by MABEL DEARMER. Small 4to, decorated cover. 4s. 6d. net. [*In preparation.*
AT THE RELTON ARMS. (*See* KEYNOTES SERIES.)

Shore (Louisa).
POEMS. With an appreciation by FREDERIC HARRISON and a Portrait. Fcap. 8vo. 5s. net.

Short Stories Series.
Each volume Post 8vo. Coloured edges. 2s. 6d. net.

 I. THE HINT O' HAIRST. By MÉNIE MURIEL DOWIE.
 II. THE SENTIMENTAL VIKINGS. By R. V. RISLEY.
 III. SHADOWS OF LIFE. By Mrs. MURRAY HICKSON.

Stevenson (Robert Louis).
PRINCE OTTO. A Rendering in French by EGERTON CASTLE. With Frontispiece, Title-page, and Cover Design by D. Y. CAMERON. Crown 8vo. 7s. 6d. net.
Also 50 copies on large paper, uniform in size with the Edinburgh Edition of the Works.
A CHILD'S GARDEN OF VERSES. With over 150 Illustrations by CHARLES ROBINSON. Crown 8vo. 5s. net. [*Second Edition.*

Stoddart (Thos. Tod).
THE DEATH WAKE. With an Introduction by ANDREW LANG. Fcap. 8vo. 5s. net.

Street (G. S.).
EPISODES. Post 8vo. 3s. net.
MINIATURES AND MOODS. Fcap. 8vo. 3s. net. [*Both transferred to the present Publisher.*
QUALES EGO: A FEW REMARKS, IN PARTICULAR AND AT LARGE. Fcap. 8vo. 3s. 6d. net.

Street (G. S.)—*continued*.
THE AUTOBIOGRAPHY OF A BOY.
(*See* MAYFAIR SET.)
THE WISE AND THE WAYWARD.
(*See* FOUR - AND - SIXPENNY
NOVELS.)

Swettenham (F. A.)
MALAY SKETCHES. With a Title-
page and Cover Design by PATTEN
WILSON. Crown 8vo. 5s. net.
[*Second Edition*.

Tabb (John B.).
POEMS. Sq. 32mo. 4s. 6d. net.

Tennyson (Frederick).
POEMS OF THE DAY AND YEAR.
With a Title-page designed by
PATTEN WILSON. Crown 8vo.
5s. net.

Thimm (Carl A.).
A COMPLETE BIBLIOGRAPHY OF
FENCING AND DUELLING, AS
PRACTISED BY ALL EUROPEAN
NATIONS FROM THE MIDDLE
AGES TO THE PRESENT DAY.
With a Classified Index, arranged
Chronologically according to
Languages. Illustrated with
numerous Portraits of Ancient
and Modern Masters of the Art.
Title-pages and Frontispieces of
some of the earliest works. Por-
trait of the Author by WILSON
STEER, and Title-page designed
by PATTEN WILSON. 4to. 21s.
net.

Thompson (Francis).
POEMS. With Frontispiece, Title-
page, and Cover Design by
LAURENCE HOUSMAN. Pott 4to.
5s. net. [*Fourth Edition*.
SISTER-SONGS: An Offering to
Two Sisters. With Frontispiece,
Title-page, and Cover Design by
LAURENCE HOUSMAN. Pott 4to.
5s. net.

Thoreau (Henry David).
POEMS OF NATURE. Selected and
edited by HENRY S. SALT and
FRANK B. SANBORN, with a
Title-page designed by PATTEN
WILSON. Fcap. 8vo. 4s. 6d.
net.

Traill (H. D.).
THE BARBAROUS BRITISHERS: A
Tip-top Novel. With Title and
Cover Design by AUBREY
BEARDSLEY. Crown 8vo, wrap-
per. 1s. net.
FROM CAIRO TO THE SOUDAN
FRONTIER. With Cover Design
by PATTEN WILSON. Crown
8vo. 5s. net.

Tynan Hinkson (Katharine).
CUCKOO SONGS. With Title-page
and Cover Design by LAURENCE
HOUSMAN. Fcap. 8vo. 5s. net.
MIRACLE PLAYS. OUR LORD'S
COMING AND CHILDHOOD. With
6 Illustrations, Title-page, and
Cover Design by PATTEN WIL-
SON. Fcap. 8vo. 4s. 6d. net.

Walton and Cotton.
THE COMPLEAT ANGLER. Edited
by RICHARD LE GALLIENNE.
Illustrated by EDMUND H. NEW.
Crown 4to, decorated cover. 15s.
net.
Also to be had in twelve 1s. parts.

Watson (Rosamund Mar-
riott).
VESPERTILIA AND OTHER POEMS.
With a Title-page designed by R.
ANNING BELL. Fcap. 8vo. 4s. 6d.
net.
A SUMMER NIGHT AND OTHER
POEMS. New Edition. With a
Decorative Title-page. Fcap.
8vo. 3s. net.

Watson (William).
THE FATHER OF THE FOREST AND
OTHER POEMS. With New Photo-
gravure Portrait of the Author
Fcap. 8vo, buckram. 3s. 6d. net.
[*Fifth Edition*.
ODES AND OTHER POEMS. Fcap.
8vo, buckram. 4s. 6d. net.
[*Fourth Edition*.
THE ELOPING ANGELS: A Caprice
Square 16mo, buckram. 3s. 6d.
net. [*Second Edition*.
EXCURSIONS IN CRITICISM: being
some Prose Recreations of a
Rhymer. Crown 8vo, buckram.
5s. net. [*Second Edition*.

Watson (William)—*continued.*
THE PRINCE'S QUEST AND OTHER
POEMS. With a Bibliographical
Note added. Fcap. 8vo, buckram.
4s. 6d. net.   [*Third Edition.*
THE PURPLE EAST : A Series of
Sonnets on England's Desertion
of Armenia. With a Frontispiece
after G. F. WATTS, R.A. Fcap.
8vo, wrappers.   1s. net.
[*Third Edition.*

Watt (Francis).
THE LAW'S LUMBER ROOM. Fcap.
8vo. 3s. 6d. net.
[*Second Edition.*

Watts-Dunton (Theodore).
POEMS. Crown 8vo.   5s. net.
[*In preparation.*
There will also be an *Edition de Luxe* of
this volume printed at the Kelmscott
Press.

Wharton (H. T.)
SAPPHO. Memoir, Text, Selected
Renderings, and a Literal Trans-
lation by HENRY THORNTON
WHARTON. With 3 Illustra-
tions in Photogravure, and a
Cover designed by AUBREY
BEARDSLEY. Fcap. 8vo.   7s. 6d.
net.   [*Third Edition.*

THE YELLOW BOOK

An Illustrated Quarterly.

Pott 4to.   5s. net.

I. April 1894, 272 pp., 15 Illustrations.   [*Out of print.*

II. July 1894, 364 pp., 23 Illustrations.

III. October 1894, 280 pp., 15
Illustrations.

IV. January 1895, 285 pp., 16
Illustrations.

V. April 1895, 317 pp., 14 Illustrations.

VI. July 1895, 335 pp., 16 Illustrations.

VII. October 1895, 320 pp., 20
Illustrations.

VIII. January 1896, 406 pp., 26
Illustrations.

IX. April 1896, 256 pp., 17 Illustrations.

X. July 1896, 340 pp., 13 Illustrations.